Bella Donna

Ruth Symes thinks the next best thing to being magic is writing stories about magic. She lives in Bedfordshire and when she isn't writing she can be found by the river walking her dogs, Traffy and Bella (who are often in the river).

Find out more at: www.ruthsymes.com

Marion Lindsay has always loved stories and pictures, so it made perfect sense when she decided to become a children's book illustrator, and she won the Egmont Best New Talent Award. She lives and works in Cambridge, and in her spare time paints glass and makes jewellery.

Find out more at: www.marionlindsay.co.uk

Bella Donna

Bella Bewitched

Illustrated by
Marion Lindsay

Piccadilly

First published in Great Britain in 2013
by Piccadilly Press Ltd,
A Templar/Bonnier publishing company
Deepdene Lodge, Deepdene Avenue,
Dorking, Surrey, RH5 4AT
www.piccadillypress.co.uk

A catalogue record for this book is available
from the British Library

ISBN: 978 1 84812 335 9

Printed and bound by CPI Group (UK) Ltd, Croydon, CR0 4YY
Cover design by
Cover illustration by Marion Lindsay

For Jasmine, Damaris and Melissa
R.S.

For Zakarias and Ruben, with much love
M.L.

Chapter 1

There are some things I'm very good at, like being a witchling and casting spells. And there are some things I'm not very good at, like maths and gym. Why, oh why, oh why does gym class have to be so hard? And what's so important about being able to walk along a beam, jump over a vaulting horse, or climb a rope hanging down from the ceiling anyway?

Of course, if I'd been allowed to use magic it would have been no problem at all. Easy peasy, in fact. I could have just flown up the rope. But even though I'm a witch – or witchling as young witches are called – I have to go to school in the real world. I'm not allowed to use magic outside Coven Road, where I live, and no one who isn't a witch is even supposed to know that I am one.

'Go on, Bella,' my teacher, Mrs Pearce, said as I clung to the rope. 'Up you go.'

Huh! I'm not Tarzan and I wasn't going anywhere. What did Mrs Pearce know? She was standing safely down there on the ground. I'd like to see her try to climb the rope instead of just telling me what to do! Couldn't she see that

I couldn't go up and I couldn't go down? The truth was I was stuck. Stuck, stuck, STUCK! I stared down at the rest of my class who were all staring up at me. Some of them had their mouths open, a few were pointing. Ellen and Rajni were trying hard not to laugh, but just about everyone else – apart from Sam and Angela and Mrs Pearce – *was* laughing.

I wished I could turn myself invisible and disappear.

'You can do it, Bella,' my best friend, Sam, said. 'Just let go with one of your hands,' my other best friend, Angela, told me. My face was red with embarrassment. I hated everyone looking up at me.

Even though I knew Sam and Angela were just trying to help, their words only made me cling to the rope more tightly. My legs were clamped around it and it was scratchy against my bare skin, but if I let go, I'd fall and I definitely didn't want to fall. Even looking down made me feel a bit woozy. The rope swung scarily to and fro if I so much as breathed.

The bell for lunchtime rang and the caretaker came in through the gym's swing doors. He saw me hanging from the rope and made a 'hmph' sort of sound. I bet he thought I was stupid for getting stuck up the rope too.

We have our lunch in the gym every day and the caretaker has to set out the tables and chairs before we can start eating. Only he couldn't do it yet because of me swinging in the middle of the room.

Mrs Pearce looked at her watch. 'We haven't

got all day, Bella,'
she said. 'Come
down now.'
But I still didn't
move. If she wanted
me to come down so
badly then she could
come up and get me!
I never wanted to
do gym again.
I hated it.
Mrs Pearce sighed
loudly. 'You shouldn't
have climbed up the
rope if you knew you
couldn't get down
again, you silly girl.'
Me? Silly? It wasn't
me being silly. It was

all Mrs Pearce's fault for expecting me to climb the rope in the first place.

I'd almost rather have been doing maths than this. I'd rather have been doing just about anything than swinging from a gym rope. This was the worst Friday ever. If only I was allowed to use magic, I could cast a tiny weeny spell and gym would be so much better.

The caretaker made loud clattering and clunking sounds as he started to unstack the chairs.

'I know what to do,' Sam said.

He and Angela ran over to the vaulting horse and pushed it until it was just under me, and then they held the rope tight so it didn't wobble and swing about.

'If you just uncurl your legs from the rope they'll touch the horse,' Sam said.

Gingerly I stretched out one leg and almost

touched the vaulting horse and then I stretched
out the other one and did touch it.

'I knew you could do it,' Sam said, smiling.

'Thanks, Sam,' I said.

Angela stretched up her hand and I took it.

'Everyone back to the changing rooms,' Mrs Pearce said, as Sam and Angela helped me down. 'Quickly – but don't run!'

'What about all this gym equipment?' the caretaker said, as we ran past him. 'I suppose I'll have to put it away myself, just like I have to do everything else around here.'

We didn't stop. He's always a bit grumpy, maybe because his nose is constantly being scratched by his bristly moustache. It makes him look like he's got a giant caterpillar stuck on his face.

'It'll be easier next time,' Angela said, as we got changed.

I shook my head. 'It won't.'

'At least you've tried climbing the rope now,' Sam said, as we ate our lunch, but that didn't help either.

'Yes,' I said, 'and I don't want to try it again, thank you very much.'

I was sure the rest of my classmates were still all secretly, and some not so secretly, laughing at me.

Angela and Sam weren't as hopeless at gym as I was. At least Angela could do a cartwheel without falling over and Sam had leapfrogged straight over the vaulting horse – without belly flopping on top of it, like me.

'We've got gym again on Monday morning,' Sam added. 'Mrs Pearce said she was going to give us a fitness test then.'

Remembering that only made it worse.

'I'll never be able to climb up that rope without getting stuck,' I said. 'And I'll never be able to jump over the vaulting horse or do a forward roll, let alone a cartwheel!'

'Yes, you will,' Sam said. 'All you need is a bit more practice. Why don't you come round to my house tomorrow afternoon and we can practise together?'

'Okay,' I said. 'Thanks.'

I'd known Sam for ever. We'd both lived in the Templeton Children's Home since we were babies. Just over a year ago, I was adopted by a lovely witch called Lilith, and went to live in Coven Road. A little while after that, Sam was adopted by Trevor and Tracey, who run our local Woodland Wildlife Centre and love animals just as much as Sam does – which is lots and lots and lots. Sam and I had always dreamt that we might find a perfect family to adopt us – our Forever Family as we called it – and both of us had, although in my case my

family was one person. Sam's the only person, who isn't a witch, who knows that I am one. I love going to Sam's house, especially now he has a puppy called Bobby, but I didn't really think that practising getting stuck up a rope a few more times was going to make the fitness test on Monday any easier.

I couldn't stop thinking about it as I walked home at the end of the day. I wished there was a way, *any* way, for me to get out of having to do it. If only I was allowed to use magic outside Coven Road.

'Wait!' a voice behind me shouted, and the next moment Verity came running up. 'What are you looking so mopey for?' she said when she saw my face.

Verity's a witchling like me and lives in Coven Road too, so we sometimes walk home together although we don't go to the same school. She's a few years older than me and very pretty with big eyes and shiny black hair.

Her mum is Lilith's sister and that makes Verity Lilith's niece and my cousin. Sometimes having Verity around can be good and sometimes it can be very bad – sometimes Verity can be nice and at other times she can be really nasty. When I first came to live in Coven Road she was very jealous and tried to get me banished, but she's made up for that since then and we're sort of friends, although I still don't completely trust her.

As we walked home down the streets I told Verity how I was dreading the fitness test on Monday and how awful the gym class had been that day and how everyone had laughed at me.

'The rope kept swinging as I tried to climb it and I thought I was going to fall off!'

Verity wasn't very sympathetic. I hadn't really expected her to be.

'If you had my natural grace you'd have no problem,' she said, spinning around like a ballet dancer. 'I could be a trapeze artist if I wanted.'

Verity might have been joking, but maybe not. She always thinks she's better than me, which she isn't, but there's no point telling her because she never listens. And she probably was better than me at gym – it would be hard not to be.

'Oooh look – they're so pretty,' Verity said, and she pointed to some tiny purple wild flowers with white spots on them, growing in a small clump at the roadside.

'Yes, they are,' I agreed.

Verity crouched down and sniffed them. 'They've got a very faint scent,' she said, and then she sneezed. 'Do you know what they're called?'

I shook my head. I'd never seen flowers quite like them before, but Lilith would probably know. We use lots of wild flowers and leaves and herbs in our spells.

'I might add some of these to my Thirteenth

Moon ceremony posies,' Verity said, as we turned into Coven Road. 'I want my ceremony to be the most magical one ever.'

'You could show them to Lilith,' I suggested. 'She might know what they are.'

I sighed. And maybe Lilith would have some ideas about my gym problem. At least she'd be more sympathetic than Verity.

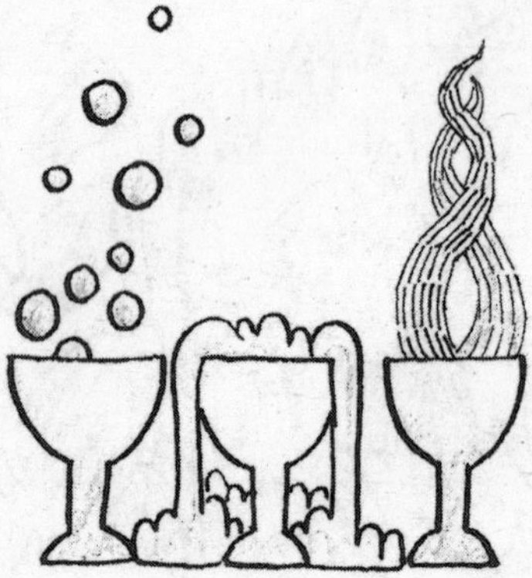

Chapter 2

There are thirteen houses in Coven Road and the people who live in them are all witches.

Although I'd always always *always* wanted to be a witch for as long as I can remember, I didn't know that I really was a witch until I met Lilith.

As soon as I saw Lilith I went all tingly with excitement because I knew she was going to be my Forever Family. I just *knew*. But I didn't know Lilith was a witch at first because you can't tell who is and who isn't a witch just by looking at them. I just knew she was the person I'd been waiting for to adopt me. Lilith has five cats – Bazeeta, Brimalkin, Amelka, Mystica and my favourite, Pegatha.

Pegatha's a small tabby cat and very funny – especially when she's jumping about trying to catch a sunbeam or racing up and down the stairs for absolutely no reason at all other than for fun. Even when I'm having a really bad day she can always make me laugh. We found out quite recently that Pegatha was actually a real witch's cat. Witches' cats are very rare, and so we are very lucky to have one. They're allowed to choose their own witch to belong to, and Pegatha could have chosen anyone at all but she chose me, and I'm not even a fully-fledged witch yet!

She's only recently discovered herself that she's a witch's cat and so she doesn't know quite how magical she'll eventually be and nor do we. But I think she'll be very magical, and perhaps even be able to speak – though at the moment she can only say one word.

'Fish, fish, fish,' Pegatha said, as she wound herself around my legs as soon as I got home.

Although Pegatha can only say one word it means lots of different things and I usually know exactly what she's trying to say.

'Yes, I missed you too,' I told her, as I picked her up. 'And I'm very glad to be home.'

I wanted to tell Lilith how worried I was about the fitness test but I didn't get a chance because Verity came home with me and all she wanted to do was talk to Lilith about her Thirteenth Moon ceremony.

Lilith smiled at me and shrugged and I grinned back as Verity talked and talked. At least I'd have Lilith all to myself once Verity had gone.

'I want my ceremony to be perfect,' Verity said. 'The most amazing ceremony there's ever been. A totally unforgettable Thirteenth Moon ...'

I couldn't blame her for wanting to talk to Lilith really. Verity's mum works really hard and often doesn't come home till late, and a witchling's Thirteenth Moon ceremony is a very big deal. If it were mine, it'd probably be the only thing I'd want to talk about too.

On the thirteenth minute of a witchling's thirteenth year, he or she gets to chant the spell that protects Coven Road from non-witch eyes for the first time. It's important that ordinary people don't find out that Coven Road is a road full of witches, so every month all the witches get together to cast a spell so that ordinary people walk right past the entrance to the road without even knowing it's there. Even if they do somehow enter the road, the spell makes it seem just like any other street with houses that all look the same – whereas really none of them are ordinary and none of them look alike. The grand sorceress, Zorelda,

lives in an ice palace that never melts. Another of the houses looks like a pirate's ship and has a skull and crossbones flag flying from the chimney. Another one is built high up in the trees.

Mr and Mrs Robson and Waggy, our next-door neighbours, have a giant spider on their roof!

Not only was Verity going to help cast the spell at precisely thirteen minutes after the time she was born, but it was also her duty to prepare all the ingredients and make the posies the witches throw into the cauldron at the end of the spell-casting. She was going to prepare the posies at our house as her mum is away a lot. It's a huge honour and a lot of hard work.

Lilith was helping Verity as much as she could, but she wasn't allowed to help her very much because the Thirteenth Moon ceremony is designed to show whether a witchling is ready to become a witch and a proper witch wouldn't have her spell-casting tutor there to help her. Verity had to prove she could do it all by herself.

'I've been practising the chant over and over, Auntie Lilith. This morning I even woke up dreaming about it,' Verity said breathlessly.

While Verity was chatting to Lilith about her ceremony, I told Pegatha all about my disastrous day at school and how I'd been stuck up in the air clinging to the rope in PE.

Pegatha looked very sweet as she sat on the sofa listening to me with her head tilted to one side. Every now and again she said, 'Fish,' to show she agreed with me or knew what I meant. She even tried to help by showing me how she could run along the back of the sofa and vault up the bookshelves and climb the curtains' cord rope.

'Yes, I know *you* can do it,' I said, laughing. 'You can do it all easy peasy – but I can't!'

Pegatha would have had no problem at all taking the fitness test that I was dreading. But she wasn't the one who had to take it, I was.

'Can you remember your Thirteenth Moon

ceremony?' Verity asked Lilith, and I turned to listen.

'Oh yes,' Lilith told her. 'No one ever forgets their Thirteenth Moon. I was terrified I'd do something wrong!'

'I want mine to be *unforgettable*,' Verity said.

Verity's Thirteenth Moon ceremony was going to be on Monday at thirteen minutes past five in the afternoon – the same day as my fitness test. I thought I probably wouldn't forget that either!

'I'd better be getting home,' Verity said, at last. 'See you in the morning.'

Once Verity had gone, Lilith gave me a hug. 'How was your day?' she asked as we went through to the kitchen to prepare supper. Lilith was making my favourite munchkin risotto while I got food ready for the cats.

'Okay, but I'm glad it's the weekend,' I said.

I'd told Pegatha all about the fitness test and I didn't feel like talking about it all over again now. But Lilith seemed to know something was bothering me.

'Is everything all right?'

I nodded.

'How about we make some popcorn after supper and watch a film?' Lilith said. 'There's a new one about witches I think you might like.'

It sounded like the perfect way to spend a Friday evening.

'Fish?' said Pegatha.

'Yes,' I told her. 'You've got fish for dinner.'

Fish is Pegatha's favourite food.

It's also Brimalkin, Bazeeta, Amelka and Mystica's favourite, and as soon as I put their bowls down they all jumped off the bookshelves – where they like to sit – to eat it.

I smiled as I watched them. They weren't worried about the fitness test and I decided I wasn't going to let worrying about it spoil my weekend either. I love weekends in Coven Road. They are when something even more magical happens.

Chapter 3

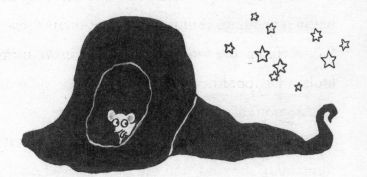

Every Saturday morning Verity and I have a spell-casting lesson with Lilith. I love casting spells and Saturdays are my absolute favourite day of the week, although I'd like them even more if Verity didn't have to be at the lessons too and it could be just me and Lilith. But Verity's the only other witchling in Coven Road, and Lilith's the only witch tutor, so Verity has to come along and that's that. Lilith is a very good spell-casting teacher as well as being a very lovely mum.

Verity knocked at our door five minutes before the spell-casting lesson was due to start.

'Morning,' she said, and then she sneezed. She looked pale and her eyes and nose were all red.

'Are you all right, Verity?' I asked her.

'No, I think I'm coming down with something,' she said, and then she sneezed again.

You might wonder why Lilith couldn't just cast a spell to make Verity instantly better, but the witches of Coven Road don't use magic for everyday things – and that includes minor illnesses. I'm not even allowed to use magic to do my homework, which I think is a shame.

Verity sneezed again.

'I better not be sick for my Thirteenth Moon ceremony,' she said.

'No,' I agreed.

I wondered if Zorelda, who's in charge of

Coven Road, would make an exception for Verity's Thirteenth Moon ceremony and cast a spell to make her better. It would be awful if Verity was sick on her special day.

Verity was holding a basket full of all the wild flowers she was thinking of using in her Thirteenth Moon ceremony posies. The really good thing about picking any flowers in Coven Road is that as soon as one is picked, another one grows straightaway in its place, unlike normal flowers. I'd never pick a wild flower outside of Coven Road though, because I know another one wouldn't grow for a long time.

'Do you think these flowers will be all right, Auntie Lilith? *Atchoo!* I found nearly all of them in Coven Road,' she said, and then she sneezed again.

'I'm sorry, Verity,' Lilith said firmly, and she turned her head away so she couldn't even see the flowers in Verity's basket. 'Don't show them to me. You know I'm not allowed to look. Take the basket outside. You don't want to be disqualified from doing your Thirteenth Moon ceremony, do you?'

No one was allowed to help Verity with choosing her flowers. Verity had to choose them all by herself. The flowers a witchling chooses for the ceremony's posies must reflect who she is and how she feels about herself. If she has help from another witch then the magic of the posies would be tainted.

From the quick glance at them I had, I could see that Verity had chosen mainly purple and white flowers, with a few red ones thrown in for dramatic effect. Verity can be very dramatic sometimes!

She quickly took the basket back outside. Although she was allowed to make her posies at

our house before the ceremony on Monday, we weren't allowed to actually help her with making them.

'Sorry, Auntie Lilith,' Verity said, when she came back. 'I didn't think. I was just so excited and wanted to show you what I'd found. Bella saw some of the flowers I'm going to use yesterday. Do you think that matters?'

'I'm sure that'll be all right,' Lilith said, and she gave her a hug. Verity looked a bit less worried. 'I know you're looking forward to your big moment, but you mustn't ask me for my help.'

'I won't, I promise,' Verity said.

'Good. Now what would you like to learn about today?'

'Can we revise the different properties of wild flowers, please, Auntie Lilith?' Verity asked her. 'It won't be

helping me exactly but it'll be useful when deciding which flowers I'd like to use.'

'Fish,' Pegatha said scornfully and I sort of agreed with her. Verity was almost asking Lilith for help, but not quite. Pegatha always came along to my spell-casting lessons and she doesn't like Verity very much.

But Verity had to choose her posy flowers

carefully so I didn't really blame her for trying to get a little help, even in a roundabout way. While the flowers she chose needed to reflect her personality, they also needed to work well together to seal the protection spell.

Some flowers, like geraniums and roses, grow best when they're planted next to each other, and so are also powerful when used together in spells. But some flowers, like lupins and tomato plants, don't grow well when they're planted next to each other and if they're both used in the same spell, the effect will be weak.

'All right,' Lilith agreed. 'Let's start with a little test to see what you can remember. What do we use smudge sticks for?'

'Cleansing and purifying the air,' Verity and I said at the same time.

'And what flowers might we put in them?'

'Lavender,' I said.

'With some sage and mugwort,' added Verity.

'Fish,' Pegatha agreed.

'And why do we use lavender?' Lilith asked.

'Because it restores balance,' I said, 'and it creates a peaceful atmosphere.'

'Well done,' Lilith said. She smiled at me and I grinned back at her.

'I knew that too,' Verity said crossly.

'I'm sure you did,' Lilith soothed.

Verity can get a bit jealous sometimes. I think it's partly because I'm really good at spell-casting even though I've not been learning for as long as her, and partly because before I came to live in Coven Road, she had Lilith all to herself. But I can't help that.

'Are there any flowers or plants that we never use?' Verity asked.

'Not really,' Lilith said. 'None of the flowers in Coven Road are actually harmful, but as you know, some compliment each other better than others. It's important that you know all the qualities of the flowers you're using in your posies.'

We discussed the properties of flowers for a bit, and then Lilith said, 'Now would you like to learn how to make a flower tonic? I know one that might help to ease your cold a little, Verity.'

'Can we make a smudge stick too?' I asked, and Lilith said we could. I love the smell when it burns!

To make our smudge stick we used sage, mugwart, rosemary and lavender from the back garden. We cut a ten-centimetre piece from each of the herbs and plants and then bound the ends together with a long piece of cotton string. Then we used the remaining length of the string to wind round the length of the bound plant pieces in a criss-cross pattern.

'Not so tightly that it damages any of the plants,' Lilith reminded us.

'Can we burn it now?' Verity asked, once it was done. But Lilith shook her head. 'This one is too new. It needs to dry out for a few days first or it won't burn.'

'Awww,' Verity said.

'Only minutes after Philippa died.' I was surprised to find that as I said it, I felt a pang of something.

'But you know it's completely different for men,' said Penny, rather crossly.

'Barbara Windsor married a man twenty-six years her junior,' I said, trying to be consoling. 'Joan Collins and what's-his-face, thirty years younger?'

'Marie, don't bullshit. You know and I know that this is going to end in tears,' said Penny with a flash of her old self. 'And the other awful thing is that because I, like you, am a sixties girl, I go straight back into that servile "yes-you're-a-man-I'll-do-anything-you-want" mode when these days all that's changed.'

'Maybe that's what he loves about you,' I said.

'Marie, I'm depending on you, during this whole disastrous caper, to be my sensible self,' said Penny. 'I rely on you to pour cold water on everything. Don't start encouraging me in my madness. Please. Though thank you,' she added, changing like Eve (as in *The Three Faces of*, the movie), getting suddenly all girlish and fluttery, 'for the KY. Oh, I can't stop thinking about him! It's awful!'

There was a pause while she stared at her empty glass. I suddenly caught on and rushed to the fridge to get the bottle to top her up. When I got back I was astonished to see tears had come to her eyes.

'You should feel happy, not miserable,' I said, putting my arm round her.

'But I know already that the relationship hasn't got a hope,' she said, rather sadly. 'You see, you've got Gene to love. But I don't have anyone.'

And I suddenly realized how selfish I'd been, always talking to Penny about Gene. It must have been much more painful and envy-making for her than it was for me hearing her talking about this bloke.

But Gavin! Glastonbury she?

Later
Pouncer has discovered the to eat them. Back to the thr

Later
Went to the shops and com by a woman in a burqa speed disabled motorized chair thi before my house and as I pass who'd obviously insulted her in th she shrieked in a strong cockney acc shroud. 'I'm more fucking En

Later
Penny rang with a query: 'V she asked.

Sep 12

Rather worried because room with a man in tow her age (but probably h stairs, but I saw that h through one ear, wa strongly of dope. Havi sixties, I have one of twenty paces. In fact shuffle round Heath suitcases for drugs.

When, later, I a

dreamy
was 'a
'Wh
piciou
'He
of gar
artist,
Th
this
reve
man
'
'
her
said
know
good.
Been
when t
some n

Sep 13th

Just read
attacks tha
Total tosh.
for me at l
go on living
I used to h
because I kn
else, he, too,
before.

There is also the bizarrely pleasurable knowledge that my family is now part of a chain. On one level I couldn't give a fuck – oh, Marie, no no no! That is not a nice word for an old person to use! All my contemporaries say it, but it just doesn't suit them – anyway, I couldn't give a pin, let's say, or a fig, whether the Sharp genes staggered on to the generation after next, but now I've discovered that they have, I feel ever so slightly smug. So smug, in fact, that I find it terribly hard to talk about Gene to anyone who either has no children or who has children but has not yet got grandchildren. I should never have told Penny how happy I am about him. It's exceptionally bad manners to gloat.

September 14th

Michelle asks, 'What means vegetation?' She swears that this is a plant-like substance that, in France, grows up people's throats and into their sinuses, and has to be cut back regularly in some patients. I simply cannot believe it. She then asks me if I know how to pronounce the film 'Beneer'.

After five tries, I look baffled.

'Beneer!' she says. 'Charlton 'Eston! Many horses!'

September 15th

Couldn't resist it. I went to John Lewis today and bought a knitting pattern.

It was my grandmother who'd originally got me started. She bought me a book called *How to Knit* published by Patons and Baldwins. The patterns were not only for socks and vests, but strange garments like mittens, pinches (?), footlets and spencers. She also bought me a pair of huge wooden needles.

She taught me how to wind the wool round my fingers so it wouldn't slip and, snuggled in the corner of her vast sofa, I would struggle to control these vast sticks which, in my small hands, seemed like two great broom handles, waving around beyond my control.

After hours of trying, I succeeded, eventually, in knitting my father a 12-foot-long lime-green scarf in secret for Christmas which he nobly wore for years. Occasionally it trailed out beneath his duffle-coat and dragged along the ground.

I had a very odd moment in John Lewis. I was looking at the carpet for some reason, which was bottle-green, and something seemed to spring out of it like that creepy thing in *Alien*, and whack straight into my heart. I think it reminded me of a bottle-green coat I once had, but it filled me with a mad and poignant mixture of comfort and nostalgia. The John Lewis staff around me must have wondered whether to put their Health and Safety strategies into operation when they saw me staring at the carpet, completely goofed out.

And then last week I saw a leaf on a bush and for some inexplicable reason it reminded me of walking to school on a hot autumn day, holding my father's hand. The tears that sprang to my eyes were inexplicably pleasurable.

Everyone tells me how they are losing their memory now they are getting older, and complain about 'senior moments' but I, on the other hand, am astonished by how much my memory has improved. The short-term's got better because I am so much less anxious than I used to be. And I also take masses of fish-oils. If fish could improve Jeeves's brain, then they can improve mine, too. But what is wonderful is the sudden gift of long-term memory. Cracks seem to appear in the walls of my consciousness, revealing glimpses of the past as clear as if they were happening in front of my eyes. Sometimes I feel intense emotions about these moments that I never, as far as I remember, felt at the time.

I was disappointed that we couldn't burn it straightaway too. I love the smells of sage and rosemary and lavender.

'We can light it at next week's class,' Lilith told us.

For the flower tonic we made a tea by adding echinacea with meadowsweet, elder-flower and some ginger root to hot water and letting it infuse.

'Smells yummy,' Verity said, as Lilith poured her a glass.

Lilith poured me one too. 'It'll help you not to catch Verity's cold,' she said. I sipped the tonic. Verity was right. It was yummy and the ginger made it warming as well.

The tonic must have worked too, because Verity was no longer sneezing.

Lilith lit a smudge stick that she'd made the week before and was now ready to burn. Verity and I took it in turns to waft it in the air and around ourselves.

'What herbs have I used in it?' Lilith asked us.

'Basil?'

'Yes.'

'Thyme?'

'Very good.'

'And lemon balm.'

'Correct. Any spices?' Lilith asked us.

Verity and I sniffed the smudge-stick-scented air.

'Cinnamon . . .'

'Vanilla and nutmeg.'

'Well done.'

The smudge stick had burnt away and our lesson was over.

'I'm going to spend the rest of the day choosing my posy flowers,' Verity said at the end of the lesson. 'I want just the right combination of magical properties

and smells, plus I want them to look very pretty as well.'

She was so excited that she rushed off without taking her basket of wild flowers with her. I didn't want them to be wasted so I took the flowers inside and put them in a vase full of water. I started to sneeze while I did it, though – I hoped I wasn't catching Verity's cold. Although I didn't mind being ill if it meant I missed the fitness test!

I took the flowers upstairs and put them in Lilith's bedroom. Lilith loves flowers and I was pleased to see that they seemed to have perked up already. The little purple ones with white spots in particular looked much better than they had before.

'Oh, they look nice,' Lilith said, and she sniffed at the flowers and then she sneezed too!

'Bless you,' I said.

'Thanks. Now what would you like for lunch?'

'Just a sandwich, please,' I said. I didn't want to be too full to move when I went to practise for the fitness test with Sam later.

Lilith made mushroom pâté salad sandwiches for lunch. She used her special homemade rosemary bread and that made them extra delicious. Because we had both been sneezing, I had some more of the flower and ginger tonic that we'd made in class, and Lilith had ginger tea.

'Is Angela going with you this afternoon?' Lilith asked me.

'No, it's just me and Sam. Did you have to do a fitness test when you were at school?'

Lilith frowned and then she nodded as she remembered. 'Well, we had to do lots of press-ups

once. I suppose that was a kind of fitness test. I didn't really like doing those.'

'I wish I could use magic to help me,' I said.

'It certainly would make it easier,' Lilith said smiling, although we both knew I wasn't allowed to do so. 'I expect your classmates would be very surprised if you were able to fly around the room on a gym mat.'

'And if the vaulting horse turned into a real horse.' I laughed.

'Indeed.'

'And the rope became a python or a tree – a tree growing right up into the gym roof.'

'Like the beanstalk in *Jack and the Beanstalk*?'

'Exactly.'

If only the fitness test could be magical, it would be so much more fun! But it wasn't.

'See you later,' I said, when we'd finished our drinks and I'd given Lilith a hug. I climbed on my bike and headed off to the Woodland Wildlife Centre to practise for the fitness test with Sam.

🕷 🕷 🕷

Tracey was busy feeding a baby fox from a bottle when I arrived. They're always doing interesting things there. I really loved it when they were looking after baby hedgehogs and let me help feed them.

'Sam and Bobby are over in the parkland,' Tracey told me. The two of them go everywhere together whenever they're allowed. Of course, Bobby can't go to school with Sam, although I bet he would if he could. Our lessons would be much more fun if Bobby came to them too!

As soon as he saw me, Bobby came racing over, his tail wagging. I've known Bobby ever

since the day he came to live at the Woodland
Wildlife Centre. I bent down to stroke him and
he jumped up and licked my face, which made
me laugh, so he did it even more!

'Bobby, her face is clean now!' Sam said, but
Bobby still gave my face one more lick before
he sat down and looked up at Sam. 'Good dog,'
Sam told him and Bobby's tail wagged even
though he was sitting down.

'Ready?' Sam asked me, and he pointed to a
tree branch that had a rope tied to it. 'I thought

it'd be best to start with something lower than the gym ceiling.'

I looked at the rope and the tree branch and told myself I shouldn't be scared. But I *was* scared. The tree branch wasn't as high as the gym ceiling but it was still high, or at least I thought it was.

Slowly I went towards it, although I'd much rather have been helping Tracey with the baby fox.

'At least if you fall it won't be as far and there's soft grass to land on,' Sam said.

And now I really didn't want to climb the rope because I knew that landing on soft grass wouldn't be soft – not really, not like landing on a mattress. It would hurt a lot.

But I'd said I'd give it a go, so I did. I took a deep breath and clasped the rope as high up as I could, lifted my feet off the ground, and locked my feet around the rope. But then I couldn't seem to slide my hands up the rope to go any further.

'Do you want me to give you a push?' Sam asked. He sounded a bit confused. Sam's always off climbing and exploring in his quest to meet as many animals and insects as possible, so he's had lots more practice than me.

'No – it's okay,' I said in a small voice as I put my feet back down on the ground.

Bobby sat and looked up at me with his head tilted to one side.

'Why don't we try climbing trees instead?' Sam said. 'It'll be

good practice for when we have to climb the wall bars.'

Bobby stayed on the ground as Sam started to climb a tree.

'Come on,' Sam called to me.

'Which branch should I start with?' I called back.

There was a choice of two, but I didn't really want to climb up either of them. I'd rather stay safely down on the ground with Bobby.

'Choosing is a bit like subconscious geometry,' Sam said.

'What?' I didn't think climbing trees was the least bit like geometry.

'You work out the distance and the angle of the branches and you climb to them, just like you do on a piece of paper in geometry, only in tree-climbing geometry you do it in your head.'

'And then I make my choice,' I said, as I

chose the branch I wanted to go to. I scraped my knee as I climbed and I was a lot slower than Sam but I managed to get halfway up the tree before I decided enough was enough.

'I'm quite comfortable here, thank you,' I called out to Sam who'd almost reached the top of the tree.

I was even more comfortable fifteen minutes later, when we were back on the ground!

'Can you stay for dinner, Bella?' Tracey asked.

I shook my head. 'I'd better be getting back,' I said. I'd had quite enough of practising for the fitness test for today.

I grabbed my bike and cycled home.

The weird thing was that although it had been sunny when I was at the Woodland Wildlife Centre, the closer I got to Coven Road the more cloudy it became. And as I turned the corner it actually started raining, which was

very unusual because more often than not it's sunny in Coven Road even when everywhere else is having bad weather.

'Not rain! It can't be raining!' Verity cried, as she came running up behind me holding two bulging bags.

'What've you been buying?' I asked her, as we ran into Coven Road. It seemed to be getting stormier by the second.

'New clothes for my ceremony,' Verity shouted over the rumbling thunder, as she shielded her hair with her bags.

When I got back to our house there were no lights on.

'Lilith,' I called out. 'Lilith, where are you?'

I heard a sneeze and then a cough, coming from upstairs. I went up to Lilith's bedroom and found her lying in bed, with Pegatha and a box of tissues beside her.

'Lilith, are you okay?' I asked her.

I didn't really need to ask because I could see that she didn't look very well at all. Her face was all pale, apart from her nose and eyes, which were very red.

'I'm fine,' Lilith said, and then she gave a giant sneeze. 'It's just a liddle dold.'

'I'll make some more flower tonic,' I said, and then I sneezed too.

'Oh no, don't say you're catching it as well,' Lilith said, and she tried to get up.

'No, no, you stay there,' I told her.

I'd never seen Lilith poorly before and I was worried. I ran to the kitchen and added extra ginger and some lemon to the tonic of elderflower, echinacea and meadowsweet. Then I poured a glass for Lilith and one for myself. Although I hadn't said so to Lilith, my throat did feel a bit tickly and scratchy.

After I'd taken Lilith her tonic, I made us some tomato and basil soup for dinner. Lilith could only manage to eat a little bit of hers.

'Do you think you could you have an allergy to something?' I asked her, but Lilith shook her head.

'I'm not allergic to anything,' she said. 'I'm sure it's just a cold.' She blew her nose and took a spoonful of her soup. 'Oh, that is nice.'

I smiled. 'There's still some left in the pot if you want more,' I said.

Lilith shook her head. 'This is quite enough, thank you. I think I'm very lucky to have such a thoughtful daughter and am feeling quite spoilt. Flowers in my room and now dinner in bed . . .'

'You're worth it,' I started to say, but then I felt a tickle in my throat and the next moment I gave a loud sneeze.

'Oh dear, I think you *must* have caught it!' said Lilith.

Chapter 4

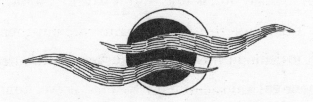

On Sunday, Lilith's cold or flu – or whatever it was – grew even worse. She spent most of the day in bed, apart from when she came downstairs and slept on the sofa instead.

My one sneeze in Lilith's bedroom hadn't

turned into a cold and I felt fine but a bit bored. I watched some Witch TV and played on the computer and looked out of the window at the pouring rain. But still I wished Sunday would go on for ever because I knew when I woke up the next day it would be Monday – the day of the dreaded fitness test. And it was first thing in the morning!

On Sunday evening I made myself and Lilith a sandwich and poured her some flower tonic. Then I gave the cats their dinner, did my homework, packed my schoolbag and went to bed. None of it was much fun without Lilith there too. And all the time I was worried about the fitness test.

'Night, Pegatha,' I said, as I pulled the covers up around my chin.

Pegatha always sleeps in my room on my bed, usually on my pillow right next to me.

She's done this ever since Lilith adopted me and I came to live here in Coven Road. I'm very pleased Pegatha likes sleeping in my room, because I love having her with me.

Pegatha purred and curled herself up into a small ball. She was soon fast asleep, but it took me much longer. I really didn't want to be stuck up the gym rope and I really didn't want everyone to be pointing and laughing at me again.

Not only did it take me ages to fall asleep, but then I woke up an hour earlier than usual. I'd heard people laughing in my dream and knew they were laughing at me.

Pegatha was still asleep so I lay very still and just watched her until she stretched and yawned and opened her little cat eyes.

'I soooo wish I didn't have to do the stupid fitness test today,' I told her.

Usually Pegatha's very good at listening to my troubles, but this morning she just blinked and then she jumped off the bed and ran out of the room.

'Pegatha!' I called after her. But she didn't come back.

I heard Lilith coughing and climbed out of bed and pushed open her bedroom door. Lilith was lying in bed with my vase of wild flowers blooming on the stand beside her.

'Don't come in,' she said from her bed as I stood in the doorway. Her throat was so hoarse she could hardly speak. 'I don't want you to catch my bug.'

'I don't mind,' I said, and then I sneezed. While I would get to miss the fitness test if I was ill, I mostly didn't want to leave Lilith when she was so poorly.

Lilith wouldn't hear of my staying home.

'No, I don't want you to miss school because of me,' she said, and then she had another coughing fit. She made a horrible wheezing sound when she coughed, like it was hard for her to breathe.

'Will you be able to get your own breakfast?' Lilith gasped, as she sank back into her pillow.

'Of course,' I said. 'And I'll bring you up some more flower tonic.'

'No, no, please don't come into my room. I don't want you to get sick,' Lilith croaked. 'I hope I don't pass it on to the witches at Verity's ceremony tonight, if I'm well enough to go. I don't want to let Verity down. Oh and Bella ...'

'Yes?'

'Good luck with the fitness test. I'm sure it won't be as bad as you think it'll be.'

I closed Lilith's bedroom door and went downstairs.

Pegatha
miaowed
loudly and I
went over to
the coffee
table where
she was
sitting on top
of Lilith's
special book
of spells.

'Fish,' she said, when I lifted her off it.

Lilith's special spell book is called a grimoire and all the witches of Coven Road have one. It's where they write all their best spells, as well as other bits and pieces. I don't have a grimoire yet because I'm not old enough, but one day, when I'm a proper witch, I will.

Pegatha hopped out of my arms and put her

paw on top of Lilith's grimoire and then looked up at me. 'Fiiiiiish.'

I knew Pegatha wanted me to look inside the book. She loves looking in the grimoire and I do too, although I'm not allowed to cast any spells from it without Lilith's permission. And Lilith prefers it if we look at the book together.

'Just a little look,' I told Pegatha, and Pegatha snuggled up to me so she could take just a little look too.

Lilith's grimoire had been passed down the generations. It had been given to her by her mother, and her mother's mother had given it to her, and so on and so on. It was very old but the paper wasn't all crumbly like a normal ancient book's paper would be.

At the front, Lilith had stuck a photo of me

and Pegatha. As I turned the pages, I passed spells to ward off bad things and make good things happen, and spells to cure ailments and fix ill wills. There were big, complicated spells that I wasn't ready to cast, and small, quick spells that I'd have liked to try – although witchlings are only allowed to do spells they've been taught and even then only under supervision.

As well as spells, the grimoire also had useful information about herbs and plants and other ingredients we use. I wondered if there was anything that might help Lilith feel a little better. I read that sage is used for cleansing and mint for energy. Lilith certainly didn't have much energy to fight off her illness, so perhaps they would be helpful.

I forgot all about getting ready for school as I looked at the book. It was so interesting.

'I expect Verity'll put some wild roses in her posies,' I said, as I looked at some pictures of them. 'They're so pretty.' But the star-like golden flowers of the coltsfoot would be beautiful too.

'Fish,' Pegatha said, as she looked at the book's
pages
intently.

Verity
must have
chosen
which
posy
flowers
she
intended

to use for the ceremony by now. But she wouldn't be using any Belladonna, or deadly nightshade as it's also known, because that's poisonous, although I'm not poisonous and my name's *Bella Donna* – although it's two words rather than one. Mrs Pearce calls me Isabella sometimes, even though she knows I like to be called Bella Donna much more.

There were some plants I'd never heard of in the grimoire's list of dangerous ones. One was called Witch's Bane and it brought sickness to any witch who breathed its scent, and misery to that witch's coven, and there was another called Jezebel's Wrath, which made everyone hate each other. Both plants were perfectly normal flowers that did no harm in the 'normal' world, but unleashed bad magic if they were brought into the witches' world. I glanced at the pictures of them – I was surprised how pretty they looked, when they could cause such problems. I hoped we didn't have either of those growing near here.

I could have spent hours poring over the grimoire and reading about the plants, but I needed to get ready for school.

Pegatha kept looking at me intently, then miaowing at me to turn the page. I turned the next page and the next. What did she want? Suddenly she put out her paw to stop me.

'*How to swap places with your familiar,*' I read.

'Fish,' said Pegatha.

'But you're not my familiar,' I told her. 'You're a witch's cat.' Familiars are spirits in animal form that help witches.

'Fish, fish!' Pegatha disagreed.

And she was right in a way. Familiars help witches and Pegatha's always helping me feel happy just by being my little cat friend. 'Fish,' Pegatha said, to remind me what I was supposed to be doing.

'All right, I'll read through the spell,' I said. It did look like a very simple one. It was also easy to reverse – all the witch and her familiar had to do was touch each other and say the spell backwards and they'd instantly be back to normal.

'Fish,' Pegatha said, and

she put her paw out again and looked at me.

'Yes, it's a good spell,' I told her, and I was about to turn the page when Pegatha stopped me.

'Fish, fish!'

I looked at Pegatha and tried to work out what she wanted.

'What is it?'

She tilted her head to the page I'd just read.

I looked down at it.

'Fiiiiish,' Pegatha said, and it sounded almost like a plea.

I still didn't understand – and then suddenly I did!

'You mean . . . ? I couldn't . . . could I? I wouldn't be allowed . . .' But Lilith was upstairs sick in bed, and there was no one to tell me what I could and couldn't do.

'You want me to cast the spell?'

Pegatha purred.

I read through the page again. It would be brilliant. Pegatha could become me and I could become her, just until after the fitness test. We'd have no trouble reversing it, and no one need ever know that the spell had even been cast!

I had a look through the ingredients.

Lavender sprig, redbush leaf, white ash, gold thread, silver flower, liquorice pearl and seven marigold seeds.

I could see almost immediately that we had all the ingredients that the spell needed to work. I bit my bottom lip.

It would be so good if I could swap places with Pegatha. Gym was the very first lesson of the day and I was really dreading having to climb up the gym rope again. What if I got stuck? I could still remember the rest of my classmates staring up at me, laughing, and Mrs Pearce looking at her watch, and the grumpy caretaker making his 'hmph' sound.

Pegatha could climb the rope easy peasy.

I wasn't supposed to use magic outside Coven Road but I'd be casting the actual spell *inside* Coven Road and it would all be over before anyone had even noticed anything unusual had happened.

'Fish?' Pegatha said.

'I'm not sure,' I said, but I really wanted to cast the spell.

Pegatha hopped out of the back door through her cat flap and came back in with a sprig of lavender in her mouth.

'Fish,' she said, dropping the lavender in front of me.

'We really shouldn't . . .'

But Pegatha didn't listen. She went back out through the cat flap and came back in with the second of the ingredients we needed for the spell: a redbush leaf.

'Fish.'

I unscrewed the top of the jar of white ash and snipped off a piece of gold thread.

We put each of the ingredients next to the cauldron, ready.

The very last thing we needed was an item belonging to each of us. Pegatha brought over a yellow ribbon toy and I found my black hair scrunchie.

'As soon as you've done the fitness test we'll swap back,' I said. Although Pegatha might be good at gym, I couldn't expect her to read and write as well. 'I'll hide in my schoolbag and you take me with you to the gym when you go to do the test.'

'Fish,' Pegatha agreed.

'Ready?'

'Fish, fish.'

I dropped all the ingredients and my hair

scrunchie into the cauldron and Pegatha dropped her yellow ribbon toy in. Then I chanted the spell three times.

'*Castilistolan mystolandia re, castilostolan mystolandia mystoldaia rah. Castilistolan mystolandia re, castilostolan mystolandia mystoldaia rah. Castilistolan mystolandia re, castilostolan mystolandia mystoldaia rah.*'

No sooner had I said the last word than Pegatha changed into me and I changed into Pegatha!

'It worked!' I cried. Or so I tried to say. But what came out of my cat mouth was, 'Fish!'

I tried speaking again, but however hard I tried all I seemed to be able to say was, 'Fish, fish, fish.' It was very frustrating.

Pegatha's mouth was opening and closing, as if she was trying to say something, and then

suddenly she said, 'Bella Donna. My name's Bella Donna.' And then she laughed and laughed. It was funny hearing her laughing. She sounded quite a lot like me but not exactly the same, at least not to my cat ears. She did look almost exactly like me, although I think I would have been able to spot whether it was me or her, if we were standing next to each other. There were tiny differences, like how she smiled and the

way she twisted her hair around her finger, which I don't usually do.

I never ever have fish for breakfast. I like to have toast or cereal or, best of all, blueberry pancakes. But this morning the fish that Pegatha put on the plate on the floor in front of me smelt sooooooo good. My head went down

and my mouth opened and before I knew it, all the fish was gone and my little rough pink tongue was licking the outside of my mouth to get every last tiny bit of fish.

Pegatha smiled. 'Cat treat?' she said, picking up a bag from the counter. 'They're fish-flavoured.'

Normally I wouldn't have found a fish-flavoured cat treat even the slightest bit tempting – but today I did.

Pegatha gave me three and I gobbled them all up and could have easily eaten more. She put the cat treat bag into my schoolbag.

'In case you get peckish later,' she said.

I thought this was a very good idea and miaowed to let her know so.

'Now what can I have for breakfast?' she said.

It was weird watching Pegatha being me. She didn't fancy eating fish for breakfast because her tastebuds were now my tastebuds. Just like I had new cat tastebuds.

Pegatha looked in the cupboard and finally pulled out a packet and poured herself a bowl of cereal and added some almond milk to it. I used to like cereal and almond milk for breakfast too – but not today.

'Yeowl!' I cried, and only just managed to stop her from putting her head down and lapping up her cereal like a cat.

Pegatha's brow furrowed as she looked at me, but then she remembered what she was supposed to do.

'Oh yes, that's what you and Lilith do,' she said, and she picked up a spoon and ate her cereal with that, although she didn't look very comfortable doing so and kept missing her mouth. 'How on earth do you manage without whiskers?' she said.

I tried to grin but my cat face didn't do grins. I thought people would look much better if they all had long whiskers like cats.

I wanted to be right by her, and the very

next moment I'd jumped up onto the counter beside Pegatha without even thinking about it. It was a high jump for a little cat – much higher than a person could jump. As a cat, I hadn't had a moment's worry about whether or not I could do it. I'd just done it!

I remembered reading how cats' whiskers are used for balance and also for measuring. Cats' whiskers are precisely the length of the narrowest width that a cat's body can squeeze through comfortably.

My new cat's whiskers were like bike stabilizer wheels on my cat's body.

I leapt down from the counter and then up onto a chair. I jumped on the sofa and ran along the back of it. I felt light and bendy and free. No wonder Pegatha liked chasing sunbeams! Racing and jumping and balancing in a cat's body was fun!

After breakfast, Pegatha went upstairs to change and clean her teeth, and when she came back down again I saw that she'd put ribbons in her hair. It made her look quite different to how I normally look when I go to school.

'Do I look pretty?' she asked me, and I told her she did, but all that came out was, 'Fish!'

'Good, and now you can look pretty too,' she said, and she tied a yellow ribbon round my tail.

I swished my tail back and forth. Girl

Pegatha certainly seemed to like ribbons a lot. Maybe cat Pegatha did too, but I'd never known that before.

It was time for us to leave. Often I ride my bike to school but Pegatha didn't want to ride it so we walked instead.

Pegatha would normally have scampered along ahead of me but she wasn't used to walking far on only two legs so I was the one doing the scampering. I liked having a tail very much, although it did feel a bit strange, and every now and again I'd forget it was there and it would surprise me.

The first person we saw was our next-door neighbour, Mr Robson, with his dog, Waggy.

'Morning,' Mr Robson said. 'How are you today, Bella Donna?'

'Fine,' I almost said. But luckily I remembered that he was talking to Pegatha and not to me.

'Very well, thank you,' Pegatha told him, and then she made a funny sound that was almost like a purr.

Waggy came running over to her but then he stopped, sniffed, sat down and whined.

I went over to him and he hopped away from me and barked.

'Don't know what's got into him,' Mr Robson told Pegatha, shaking his head. 'Now your cat's being friendly for once, he acts like he's never even met her before.'

At Coven Road we have our very own witch

postman because the road can only be seen by witches and a normal postman would never find it.

We were just turning the corner when our Coven Road postman arrived and turned from looking like an ordinary postman, who

rode his bike to deliver letters, into a magical postman who preferred to deliver letters via a magic carpet.

'Morning, Bella Donna,' he called to Pegatha. 'On your way to school?'

'Yes,' Pegatha told him.

I smiled my cat smile. Everyone thought she was me and I was her.

Just before we went into school, I jumped into my schoolbag so no one would know I was there. Now I couldn't wait for the fitness test to begin!

Chapter 5

'Wow, your hair looks so pretty,' Angela said to Pegatha as soon as we walked into the classroom. I wasn't very comfortable in the schoolbag because it had old crinkly sweet wrappers in it and a sharp pencil that dug into me. But luckily I could peep out through the gap in the zip. Angela looked like a giant.

'Thanks,' Pegatha said to Angela. 'I like ribbons.'

'Me too.'

I wanted to tell Angela how Pegatha and I had swapped places – and that my hair would be back to looking how it normally did tomorrow.

But I didn't. Firstly because I could only say the word 'fish', and secondly because I'm not allowed to tell Angela – or anyone else at school – that I'm really a witch.

I thought it would be best if I stayed hidden inside my schoolbag. It would be okay for Angela and Sam to see me but if all the rest of the class did too it might cause a few problems. We certainly weren't supposed to bring animals to school.

Plus, Mrs Pearce is allergic to cats and I was sure she wouldn't be pleased to find one in her classroom.

'Morning, everyone,' Mrs Pearce said, as she came into the classroom, but then she started sneezing. '*ATCHOO!* Oops, sorry, everyone. *Atchoo!*'

Her sneezing reminded me of Lilith. I hoped she was feeling a little better at home. I hadn't liked her nasty wheezy cough this morning and I knew how much she wanted to attend Verity's ceremony. Verity would be really disappointed if she wasn't there.

'Sorry, it's my allergies,' Mrs Pearce said.

'But there aren't any cats here,' I heard Sam say.

'I know, but I'm allergic to a few things,' Mrs Pearce said, and then she sneezed again. That was lucky. If she was only allergic to cats she might have been suspicious.

'Is everything all right, Bella?' Sam asked Pegatha.

'Yes, why?' Pegatha said.

'There's something different about you,' Sam

said. 'I can't quite put my finger on it.'

'It's her hair,' Angela told him. 'Her hair's different.'

'I like ribbons,' Pegatha said.

But Sam frowned and shook his head. 'It's not that. It's something else.'

Sam knows me better than just about anyone else and he isn't easily fooled. One of the things I like about him is how he keeps on believing what he knows to be right even when everyone else

around him tells him he's wrong. Now he was sure there was something was different about me and, of course, there was.

Pegatha tried to tell him. 'It's because —' But then Mrs Pearce clapped her hands for silence and Pegatha stopped talking.

'Right, everyone, off to the gym. There's no time to waste,' Mrs Pearce said.

Pegatha picked up her bag with me hidden inside it. It was time for the fitness test.

'Leave your bag here, Bella, like everyone else,' Mrs Pearce told Pegatha. Pegatha hesitated for a moment, but then she put the bag with me inside it back down again and followed the rest of the class out of the room. 'Last one out close the door, please,' Mrs Pearce called behind her.

I jumped out of the bag and ran to the door after them, but I was too late. The door closed with a click. All the windows in the classroom were shut and now I had no choice but to wait until someone opened the door before I could go out. I'd really wanted to watch Pegatha taking the fitness test, and see how impressed everyone was, but it looked like I wasn't going to be able to now.

'Fish,' I said, feeling sorry for myself.

I ate a fishy cat treat and then another one and another. They really were yummy.

I was just finishing crunching up my fourth

one when the classroom door opened and Pegatha was standing there in her gym kit.

'Quick!' she said, and I stopped eating my cat treats and ran out of the classroom and down the corridor to the gym after her, my yellow ribbon waving on my tail.

Chapter 6

The rest of the class were busy stretching and warming up for the fitness test as Pegatha pushed open the swing door to the gym, and I slipped in behind her. I jumped up onto the stage and hid behind the long red velvet

curtains. Now I could see everything and no one would even know I was there.

'*Atchoo!*' sneezed Mrs Pearce, and she held a

tissue up to her nose. 'My allergies are being such a nuisance today.'

Pegatha went to stand next to Angela, but when Angela asked her if she'd done her maths homework Pegatha just looked blank. I thought it was lucky we'd be swapping back soon because now Angela was looking confused.

'What's wrong?' I heard her whisper to Pegatha. Cats have very good hearing, much better than people's. But Pegatha didn't get a chance to reply.

Mrs Pearce looked down at her clipboard.

'Now who shall we start with? I think . . . Bella, as we don't want to run into lunchtime again. I think we'd better have you first.'

'Okay,' said Pegatha. 'What shall I start on?'

'How about the rope?' Mrs Pearce said, and Sam put his hand up to his mouth. I could see he was worried, but Pegatha wasn't.

She whizzed up the rope a hundred times faster than anyone else in the class was able to, but then she decided to show off and stretched herself out to make a star shape.

'Oh my goodness, Bella,' said Mrs Pearce, between sneezes. 'That really is quite amazing. It's so advanced, I don't think it's even on my list.'

Next, Pegatha just about flew down the rope, cartwheeled over to the vaulting horse, then forward flipped over it and walked on her hands along the beam before twirling round and round on the parallel bars.

Pegatha never usually does cartwheels or forward flips or walks on her hands because cats can't do those things – she was obviously making the most of being able to do them now in her new girl body!

'I've never seen anything like it,' Mrs Pearce

gasped. 'What an improvement, Bella! You must have been practising for hours.'

Which of course I hadn't been doing at all – apart from at the Woodland Wildlife Centre with Sam. Pegatha was just showing off, like she does at home sometimes.

'What's next, Mrs Pearce?' Pegatha asked, and Mrs Pearce looked down at her clipboard.

'Wall bars,' she said.

The next moment Pegatha was racing up the wall bars, and then crab-walking across them before hanging from them by her fingertips.

I was so busy watching her being me – only a super agile, bouncy, light-as-a-feather me, with no fear of heights – that I didn't even notice the grumpy caretaker until he was right behind me. By then it was too late.

As Pegatha swung upside down with one foot hooked through a wall bar, his big hands

grabbed me. Even though I twisted and turned and tried to scratch him and bit at his hands, no one could hear my cries over the claps and oohs and aahs of my classmates who were all watching Pegatha in awe.

'Got you!' he said.

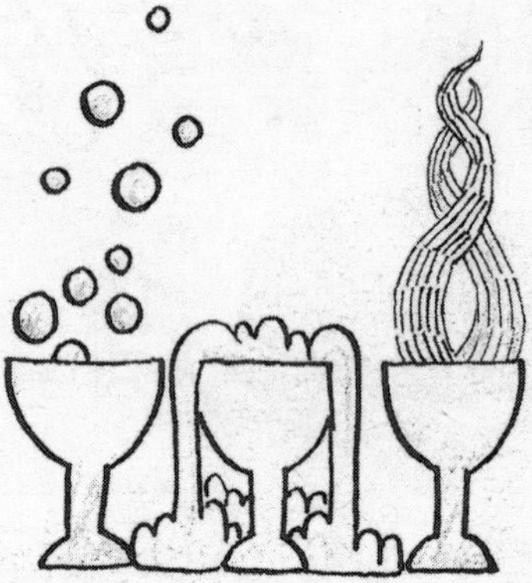

Chapter 7

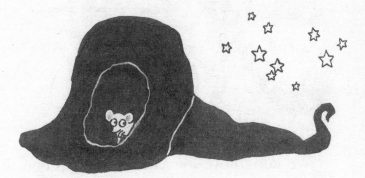

'In you go,' the caretaker said, when we'd got back to his cupboard-sized room. He tried to put me inside a cardboard box, but I wasn't going to cat prison without a fight.

I hissed at him as he sucked at the long

scratch I'd made on his hand, but he didn't listen to my hiss and I didn't dare to say the one word I could say because he would probably never let a talking cat go!

'We can't have lost cats running round the school,' he said crossly.

I wriggled desperately and tried my hardest to get away. I needed to find Pegatha and swap back. She couldn't be me for a whole day – everyone would know something was wrong. She wasn't a girl, she was a cat! But the caretaker held on tight and wouldn't let me go. I was only a little cat and the caretaker's hands were very big and strong. He put me in the box and taped the lid closed.

'You'll be safe in there,' he said.

I yeowled in protest and misery, and scratched at the sides of the box with my claws, but it was no use. Luckily there were two round fingerholes cut into two sides of the box and I stretched up and peered out of one of them.

My eyes narrowed as I watched the caretaker from my cat prison.

He took a small silver comb from his pocket. It was much smaller than the ones people use to comb their hair. I could hardly believe it when he started combing his moustache with it! I didn't even know there was such a thing as a moustache comb until then. But there was, and the caretaker spent a long, long time combing his moustache with it – or at least it seemed like a long time to me.

When he'd finally finished combing, he checked how his moustache looked in a small hand mirror. Then he took out a pair of nail scissors and snipped at his moustache before finally putting a little bit of wax from a tin on it to smooth it out.

'No rest for the wicked,' he sighed, as the bell rang.

I thought he was a wicked, mean and nasty man for trapping me and I snarled at him as he opened the door, turned off the light and went out of the room. But he didn't seem to care.

It was very dark once he closed the door and I knew I was well and truly trapped when I heard him turn the key in the lock on the other side.

There wasn't even a window for me to climb out, if I *could* manage to escape my cat prison. Pegatha would have no chance of finding me now! How were we going to swap back? Pegatha didn't even know where I was.

I waited in the darkness for a very, very long time and as I waited,

I thought about Lilith and home and wondered if I'd ever go back there again. If only Lilith hadn't been so ill then I would never have cast the spell that had changed Pegatha into me and me into her. I'd have been able to tell Lilith how worried I was about the fitness test and she'd have been able to help in some way – she'd probably have reassured me that it wasn't as important as I thought it was. It was just a test after all. But I hadn't given her a chance to do so.

My eyes closed and I felt drowsy. I couldn't help myself. It was warm and dark in the caretaker's room and cats like to have lots of naps.

As I began to doze off, I thought about how Mrs Pearce kept sneezing because of her allergies. It was amazing how she had started sneezing immediately once there was a cat around,

whereas colds come on more gradually with a tickly throat. That made me think of Lilith. Her sneezing had started quite suddenly too. Perhaps it wasn't a cold, but an allergy after all.

I thought harder. She had only started sneezing when I put Verity's wild flowers in her room. And Verity had sneezed too when she sniffed them and I'd sneezed whenever I went into Lilith's room. We hadn't got sick like Lilith, but then the flowers weren't next to us for hours and hours on end.

But Lilith had said she didn't have any allergies that she knew about, and all the flowers in Coven Road were magic. They wouldn't cause any harm. But then I suddenly remembered something. Those little purple and white flowers were the same as the ones we had seen growing

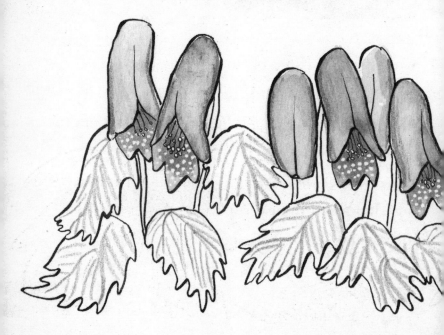

just outside of Coven Road – and Verity had said she wanted to add those to her posies. Maybe Lilith was allergic to those flowers.

And then I had a nasty feeling in my tummy and got very worried. Lilith had said that none of the flowers in Coven Road were harmful, but I'd read about some dangerous ones in her grimoire just that morning. Those sorts of flowers would never grow *in* Coven Road – but they could grow *outside* it.

I thought back to what I'd read in the grimoire. I'm rubbish at remembering most things, but I do have an amazing memory when it comes to witch things. I remembered that Witch's Bane causes sneezing — and misery! And then I remembered seeing the picture of Witch's Bane, and thinking how pretty it was. I suddenly realised that it looked very similar to the flowers that I'd put in Lilith's room . . .

My eyes flashed open and I wasn't the least bit sleepy any more. The more I thought about it, the surer I became that Verity had accidentally picked Witch's Bane, and I'd

accidentally put it in Lilith's room. And if Verity used the flower in the posies in her Thirteenth Moon ceremony, then all the

witches of Coven Road
would get sick too!
Plus it might mean Verity
failed the Thirteenth
Moon ceremony, and even though Verity could
be very annoying, I didn't want that to happen.
Well, actually, if I was really honest, a teeny
little part of me did – but luckily the nicer part
of me knew how awful it would be.

I was more desperate than ever to get out of
my cat prison and back to Coven Road.

But what was I going to do? What *could* I do
trapped in a cardboard box? I wished I could
cast a spell to get me out of this mess. But even
if I knew a spell I could cast, I couldn't do
anything while I was a cat. It was hopeless and
every minute felt as long as an hour in the
darkness. I desperately needed Pegatha to find
me, so we could swap back.

Verity's Thirteenth Moon ceremony was taking place at thirteen minutes past five and whenever a ceremony takes place, the magic of Coven Road, both good and bad magic, is much stronger than usual. I had to get back there before it was too late. I had to!

I scratched and gnawed at my cat prison but it was no good – I couldn't get out.

Then I heard the sound of a key in the lock. I hoped it was Pegatha coming to rescue me. The light was switched on and my heart sank. It wasn't Pegatha – it was the caretaker.

He picked up the cardboard box, with me inside it, and by peeking through the holes I realised he was carrying me outside and across the playground, and then he put me inside a white van and left me there.

Ten minutes later, there was the ring of the bell for the end of school followed by the sound of lots of children laughing and shouting to each other as they headed for home.

I wished I could have been going home too and wasn't stuck in a dusty old van. I wished I'd never thought of swapping places with Pegatha and I hoped she was all right, although I certainly wasn't all right myself. Cats can't cry, but if they could I would have been crying. What was going to happen to Lilith? What was going to happen to Coven Road?

And how had Pegatha managed to do maths in the afternoon? She'd only ever held a pencil in her mouth before, so how would she be able to write?

Outside the caretaker's van I suddenly heard two children talking. They had voices I recognised. It was Sam and Angela!

'What do you think's got into Bella?' Sam said.

'I don't know, but she's been acting really weird all day,' Angela replied. 'Although I do like how she's done her hair today. She looks so pretty.'

'But how did she suddenly get to be so good at gymnastics?' Sam said. 'It doesn't make sense. Something's definitely wrong.'

'What I can't understand is why she tried to go to sleep on her desk. She must have known Mrs Pearce wouldn't like it, especially after she'd caught her scribbling in her book instead of writing in it,' Angela said, and then she laughed. 'Although Bella did look very cute all curled up and making little purring noises.'

Because it wasn't really me, it was Pegatha, I wanted to tell them. Pegatha always has an afternoon nap.

'But it's not like her, is it?' Sam said, and he sounded genuinely worried. 'It's like Bella's been bewitched.' *You're right!* I wanted to tell him. *I am bewitched, only I bewitched myself because I was the one who cast the spell.*

Sam is the only one outside Coven Road who knows that I'm really a witchling and he's promised to never tell anyone the truth about me. Now he sounded really worried, but Angela thought he was just joking and laughed.

I howled and yeowled and miaowed and even risked saying,

'Fish,' but they didn't realise it was me inside the caretaker's van.

'And why did she run off so fast as soon as the bell rang?' Angela asked.

'I don't know, but she was worried about something. I asked her what was wrong but she wouldn't tell me,' Sam said. 'And I'm sure I heard her say, "Where are you, Bella?" It just didn't make sense.'

'It is weird,' Angela said, 'but then Bella Donna can be a bit weird sometimes – in a *nice* weird sort of way. But today it's in a bit of a *weird* weird sort of way!'

Angela would certainly think I was a bit weird if she could see me in my new cat body!

'What are you two doing near my van?' the caretaker said in his gruff voice.

'Nothing,' said Sam.

'Just going,' said Angela. 'Come on, Sam.'

I yeowled at them not to leave me but I couldn't hear them speaking any more so I knew they must have gone.

The caretaker slammed the driver's door so hard it made the whole van shake when he got in.

'Now let's get you sorted out,' he said over his shoulder as he started the engine.

I didn't know where he was taking me, or what he intended to do, but I was very, very frightened.

Chapter 8

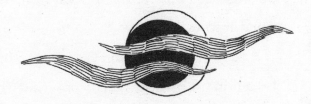

Five minutes later the caretaker's van came to a juddering stop. I crouched low in my cat prison as he got out and slammed the door shut. I was shaking with fear. I didn't know where I was or what was going to happen to me now. Poor, sick

Lilith didn't even know I'd changed myself into a cat. She'd probably guess when she saw Pegatha – if she wasn't too ill.

All I wanted was to be back home with her. I wished I'd never cast the spell. It had seemed like an easy solution to my problems but it had turned into a disaster.

And worse, if I couldn't go home then I couldn't stop the ceremony. And if I didn't stop the ceremony, then Lilith might never get better.

The back door of the van creaked open and the caretaker's hands reached in.

'This way,' I heard him say.

The cat prison bumped and shook as the caretaker walked along a pathway and then up some steps before knocking at a door. My heart was beating very, very fast. I didn't know where I was going, but I was sure I didn't want to go there, wherever it was.

'Hello, may I help you?' a friendly voice asked. It sounded like the person was smiling as they spoke, but I couldn't see who the voice belonged to from inside my cat prison.

'Wondered if you'd got space for one more,' the caretaker said, and he didn't sound as grumpy as he usually did. 'I found this cat wandering about at the school. It obviously belongs to someone because it's got a yellow ribbon tied around its tail and it seems well looked after, but it must be lost. I bet whoever's lost it is worried sick. I would be. I'll put some notices up, but they're quite likely to come to you if they've lost a cat. I'd look after it myself but I'm not allowed animals in my flat.'

'I always have space for more cats,' the voice replied, and I was sure I'd heard it somewhere before. 'I'll let the authorities know and see if anyone's reported a cat missing.'

The caretaker handed me and my cat prison over to the other person and then he went away. I couldn't believe it! I'd been so frightened but all he'd been doing was trying to help me.

The new person took my cat prison inside and set it down on the carpet.

'Now, let me have a look at you,' the voice said, and the next moment my cat prison was opened. I stared at the open top, but for a moment I was too frightened to leap out.

Then I heard a mewling coming from one side of me and a purr coming from the other. There were other cats here too.

'Now, then, I won't hurt you.'

I peeped out of my cat prison to find someone I'd met before, looking in. It was Amelia Bastet! I was at the Bastet Cat Home! Once Pegatha had got lost and she had ended up here. Lilith and I had met Amelia when we'd come here to get her back.

'Pegatha!' She smiled, recognising me immediately.

'Miaow?' I said.

Amelia was very pleased to see me – or Pegatha, as she

thought I was. She scooped me up in her arms and hugged me to her.

'It's been such a long time,' she said. 'I've thought about you so often.'

I wanted to tell her everything that had happened but I couldn't. I could only say one word, and I couldn't even say that because Amelia wasn't a witch and she wasn't magical. Not that her cats cared about that. She was better than magic for the cats who made their home with her because Amelia Bastet loved them all.

Now I was free of the cat prison, I could see that there were happy cats everywhere. It was funny, and a little bit scary, being the same size as a cat. One ginger cat put its nose up close to my nose before hopping up onto the sofa. Lots of the cats were sleeping on cushions and in sunny spots on the windowsill. Cats love to sleep! A grey and white cat came up to me, then hissed and ran away. Perhaps it knew I wasn't really a cat but a girl.

'Are you hungry?' Amelia asked me as she stroked me. 'I bet you're hungry. Let's see if we can find you something nice to eat.'

She stood up and carried me into the kitchen where there was a very old black cat with a

white star on its forehead, lying on a cushion.

'Look who's come to see us,' Amelia said to the old cat. 'It's Pegatha.'

But the old cat wasn't fooled. It knew I wasn't really Pegatha and, although it sniffed at me, it wasn't as pleased to see me as Amelia was.

'However many cats come and go there's somehow always been more than enough cat food for all of them ever since you came to stay,' Amelia said.

I gave a little cat smile. When Pegatha stayed here she made some cat food magically appear and it sounded like it had never run out.

I looked at the cat-shaped clock on the wall. It was almost time for Verity's ceremony to start. I had to get home to Coven Road – there was no time to lose.

'And it's always fish-flavoured,' Amelia said, as she put a bowl down in front of me.

It smelt delicious but I didn't have time to try it. I knew my way back to Coven Road from here and I hopped through the cat flap and raced for home as fast as I could.

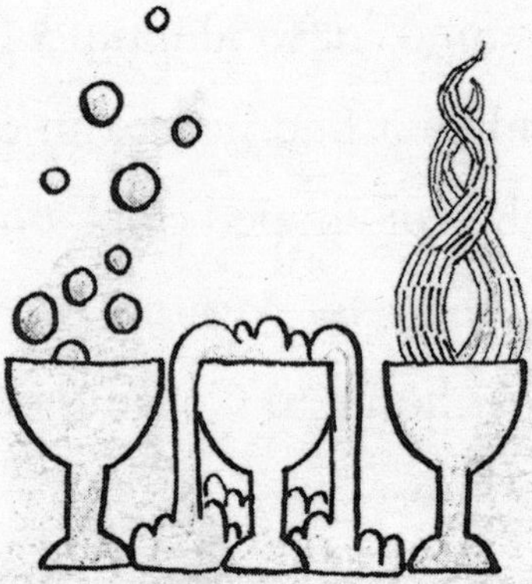

Chapter 9

One of the many differences between being a cat and being a girl is that cats don't have to stick to footpaths. Cats can hop onto fences and run through people's gardens, and no one minds a bit – which they probably would if they

found a girl running along their washing line.

Or rather, most *people* didn't mind me using their back wall as a short cut – but some pets minded very much indeed. A dog ran at me, barking at the narrow wooden fence I was running along, and I had to jump onto a

garden shed roof and scuttle down a drainpipe. Then a cat chased me as I leapt from one garden fence to the next and there was no time to try to show her I meant no harm.

Usually I'd never have been able to jump from garden fence to garden fence, or leap onto sheds. But in Pegatha's body I could do it easily. I felt different, more flexible and lighter. It was as if my cat body was one with me and I knew I could trust it and it wouldn't let me down. As soon as I'd thought of where and how I wanted to move, I'd done it. The thought that I couldn't do a movement I wanted to do didn't even enter my head.

It was much quicker getting home as Pegatha, along walls and through back gardens, than it ever was as myself. But all the way I was worrying that I wouldn't get back before Verity started to make her posies at our house.

Please don't let me be too late, please don't let me be too late, please don't let me be too late, I kept thinking over and over as I ran.

Ahead of me I saw a girl running too but then I realised it wasn't just *any* girl. It was Pegatha!

'Fish!' I called out. 'Fish!'

Pegatha stopped and came running back to me. 'I've been looking everywhere for you,' she said. I jumped into her arms and she chanted the spell we'd used to swap places, only she said it backwards this time.

'*Nalotsilitsac aidnalotsym er, nalotsolitsac aidnalotsym aiadlotsym har . . .*'

'Thank goodness we found each other,' I

said, as I transformed back into myself and Pegatha turned back into being my cat.

'Bella!' a voice called out. It was Sam and he had his puppy, Bobby, with him. 'Bella, are you okay? I was worried about you at school today.'

'I am now,' I said, 'but there's no time to waste. We have to stop Verity and help Lilith before it's too late.'

As the three of us ran towards Coven Road the sky grew darker and stormier and it started to rain. By the time I'd told Sam all that had happened we were soaked through. Worse, despite the torrential rain I could see that the usually radiant flowers in the garden at the centre had wilted and the leaves on the trees had turned brown.

'Hurry!' We all ran as fast as we could, and burst in through the front door.

Verity was sitting on the floor

surrounded by the flowers she was intending to use in her posies, and among them I recognised the Witch's Bane.

'Stop!' I shouted at Verity, as she stretched out a hand to pick up a flower.

'What? Why?' Verity said, and then she sneezed. Her eyes looked red, as if she'd been crying, but I suspected it was the Witch's Bane that was making them red and itchy.

At that moment, the grand sorceress, Zorelda, arrived. She'd obviously come to see if Verity was ready for the ceremony.

'What are you doing, Bella Donna?' Zorelda demanded to know. 'And why are Sam and that dog here?'

Sam's the only non-witch who can see the real, magical Coven Road and is allowed to come in without permission, but he'd never usually be at one of our ceremonies.

I didn't want Verity to be in trouble for using the Witch's Bane but Zorelda had to be told.

'It's an emergency!' I said. 'Verity, you're about to put a dangerous flower in your ceremony posies – I'm sure it's Witch's Bane.'

Zorelda looked at the flowers carefully and I heard her gasp in horror as she started sneezing too. 'You're right – it is Witch's Bane,' she said. 'The flower is incredibly rare. No one's seen one for years. The damage it could do to this coven is . . .' And Zorelda shuddered. I knew then how serious the situation was. Zorelda was one of the calmest people I'd ever met, and if she seemed worried then Witch's Bane must be really dangerous. 'Grey skies and dying flora are only the beginning. Quick, Sam,' she said. 'Witch's Bane is only harmful to witches, so it won't hurt you. Take it out of Coven Road, where it can't do any more harm.'

Sam quickly collected up all the purple and white flowers as fast as he could. 'Got it.'

'There's more in Lilith's room,' I said.

Sam ran upstairs and came down with the flowers from Lilith's room too, and then he and Bobby ran out of the house with it.

When Lilith came out of her room, she looked even worse than when I'd left for school – so poorly I wanted to cry.

'I'm very sorry,' I said, as I ran to her and hugged her. 'I put Witch's Bane in your room by mistake. I didn't know it was Witch's Bane when I put it in your room. I'd never have put it there if I had.'

'Shhh, it's all right, I know you didn't mean me any harm,' she said.

I ran to find the cleansing smudge stick, lit it and wafted it around her. I hadn't meant to but I'd caused her harm anyway and I felt so guilty.

The smudge stick seemed to be working and a few moments later Lilith returned to her normal self. It was like she'd never even been sick.

'I'm so glad you're okay,' I said.

'So am I,' Lilith said. 'I thought I just had a very, very bad cold. I didn't realise it was

Witch's Bane, and the more ill I became the less I could think clearly. Everything was foggy. Thank goodness you weren't badly affected by it too. And thank goodness for the smudge stick to take the last of its power away.'

'I'm so sorry I put it in your room,' I said again.

'At least now we know that although it's rare it can crop up and cause havoc,' Zorelda said. 'We must warn all the other witches that it's growing close to Coven Road, and tell them what it looks like.'

Everyone was relieved, apart from Verity.

'My Thirteenth Moon ceremony is ruined,' Verity said.
'And I wanted it to be so special.
I bought this new purple dress
and everything. Now I've failed!'

'Of course it isn't ruined,

and you haven't failed,' Zorelda told her. 'Hurry up and finish your posies with the flowers that are left. Bella Donna isn't a full witch yet so her help won't count against you.'

I hurried to help Verity make her posies and we'd only just finished as the clock struck ten minutes past five. We had three minutes to run through the rainbow-filled sky to the giant cauldron where all the other Coven Road witches were waiting, and hand the posies out.

We made it just in time. Verity took a deep breath to calm herself and then she raised her arms above her head.

'*Azhelma makara resanza del . . .*' Verity chanted once. '*Azhelma makara resanza del . .*' she chanted a second time. '*Azhelma makara resanza del . . .*' she chanted for the third time.

At the end of the chant, everyone threw their posies into the cauldron. Coven Road was

protected once again. Verity's Thirteenth Moon ceremony was over.

'Thank you for such a beautiful ceremony, Verity,' Zorelda said. 'Your posies were very pretty and they include a very good selection of flowers.'

Verity beamed with happiness and when

Pegatha went over to her and purred she smiled even more, because Pegatha doesn't usually purr at her. She bent down and stroked her, and Pegatha, for once, let her.

Zorelda smiled, and then turned to speak to the witches who were still standing around the huge caludron. 'Remember, we must only ever use flowers grown inside Coven Road for our protection spells,' Zorelda said. But she didn't tell any of the witches how close the spell had come to disaster.

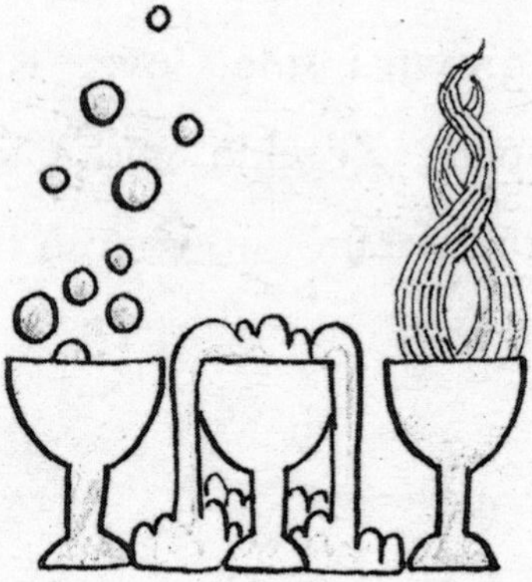

Chapter 10

After the ceremony it was time for the celebration party. Witches love parties and we're always having them because we have so many things to celebrate.

'It was very clever of you to guess we had

Witch's Bane in our midst,' Zorelda said, as Sam and Bobby came back to join us. 'It's so rare that very few witches know what it looks like. If you hadn't realised in time then who knows what might have happened?'

'I had lots of time to think about it when . . .' I started to say, before I managed to stop myself.

'When you were a cat and locked in your school caretaker's cupboard?' Zorelda said, and she raised one eyebrow and looked at me with her sharp blue eyes.

'You were a cat at school?' said Sam, and then his eyes shone with understanding. 'You were Pegatha – and Pegatha was you! That's why you seemed so different at school today!'

'Are you intending to keep swapping places with Pegatha?' Zorelda asked me.

'Oh no,' I said, as I remembered being trapped in the box and all the fishy treats I'd eaten. The thought of them made me feel a bit sick now. 'It was just that I saw the spell in Lilith's grimoire. I won't ever do it again.' Although I had liked my whiskers and how athletic I'd become.

'Good, then we'll say no more about it – this time,' Zorelda said. 'And, of course, you won't be casting any more spells from Lilith's grimoire without her permission.'

I shook my head. I wouldn't be. I felt bad that I'd made Zorelda cross. She's very frightening, especially when she's cross. I stared at the ground.

'But if you hadn't,' she continued, 'you wouldn't have recognised the Witch's Bane, and we would all have been in very serious trouble. So in some ways, we should thank you.'

I looked at Zorelda, but she had already turned to Sam. 'And Sam . . .'

'Y-yes?' Sam said. He's even more nervous around Zorelda than I am.

'Well done for looking out for your friend. The more I get to know you, the more I appreciate how lucky Bella is to have such a good friend.'

'Th-thanks,' Sam stammered, as his face went red.

Bobby ran over to Zorelda and she stroked him.

'What a fine little dog you are,' she said

laughing, as Bobby's tail wagged and wagged.

Waggy's tail also wagged happily when he saw Bobby at the party. Our neighbours' dog is usually the only dog at our witch parties but not this time. And Bobby seemed just as pleased to see Waggy as Waggy was to see him. Especially when Waggy showed him how to bark at the magic buffet table to get a bone.

I liked being back to myself and I think Pegatha liked being back to herself too. She was wearing a pink ribbon on her tail and another one round her neck. Now that I knew she liked ribbons so much I'd let her choose ones to wear

at the party as a thank you for her help – but, of course, one wasn't enough!

She hadn't eaten any fish all day when she was being me but now she ran to the magic buffet table and said, 'Fish!'

Verity looked lovely in her purple dress and top hat. Because it was her birthday as well as her Thirteenth Moon ceremony day she got lots of presents and a special witch's-hat-shaped cake.

'Happy birthday,' I said, as I gave her the amber necklace Lilith and I had bought her.

'Thanks,' Verity said.

The way she said it made me wonder if she was thanking me for more than just her present. But it's hard to tell with Verity sometimes.

After we'd had some of Verity's witch hat birthday cake, Sam and I flew round the trees on a magic carpet and petted the unicorns that live in the magical garden at the centre of Coven Road.

'How did you know Pegatha wasn't me?' I asked Sam.

'I don't know,' Sam said, as a baby unicorn nudged him for a stroke. 'I just knew.'

I smiled. It was good to have a friend like Sam. Someone who knew me through and through. But I had a surprise for him.

'Look what I can do,' I said, and I climbed up the flower rope of one of the magic swings and looked down at him from the very top.

His face was a picture!

I felt much more confident and happy doing gym sorts of things now. It had been easy doing gym-like things in Pegatha's body – but Pegatha had still been brilliant at gym when she'd only had my body. I realised maybe it wasn't just to do with what body I had, but what was in my head. I could climb the rope now, because I believed I could do it –

I just knew it — whereas before I hadn't really thought I could. It was like I knew I could do it now and so I could do it.

We fed the unicorns and then flew back to watch the Broomstick Riders' display. Before I knew it, it was almost the end of the party

and time for Sam to go home.

'See you at school tomorrow, Bella,' he said.
'You might get some funny looks – you were
being so odd yesterday!'

'Thanks for all your help, Sam,' Lilith said, as
we waved goodbye.

I was so glad everything had gone back to normal, but most of all that Lilith was better.

When we got home, Pegatha curled up on my pillow just like she always does.

'Night, Pegatha,' I said as I stroked her.

And for once Pegatha didn't say 'Fish' back, because she was already fast asleep. Well, it had been a very long and eventful day!

Chapter 11

The next day I went to school as myself, and Pegatha stayed at home and slept on the windowsill in the sun.

'Where've all your ribbons gone?' Angela said, and she sounded disappointed. 'I liked how

you did your hair yesterday. It was very pretty.'

'I think Bella's hair looks better without all the ribbons,' Sam said, and he winked at me and I grinned back.

I thought I'd have lots of explaining to do and had been trying to think of what I could

say when people
asked me why
I'd tried to go to
sleep on my desk
and why I'd
scribbled instead of written in my notebook.

But the strange thing was that no one did ask me.

There were still a few people in my class who hadn't completed the fitness test the day before so we all headed back to the gym so they could finish it. The caretaker was there, clattering around, as he stacked up some chairs.

'That's a nice moustache,' I said to him. I'd never really spoken to him before, but now I knew that although he looked a bit grumpy he was a kind man.

His hand went to his moustache and he looked a bit shocked.

'It takes a lot of work to keep a moustache looking this good,' he told me.

I almost said, 'I know,' but I just managed to stop myself in time.

'Let's start with you, Bella,' Mrs Pearce said, as she looked through the forms on her clipboard.

'But . . .' I said.

'And no getting stuck up that rope again. Only climb as high as you feel comfortable,' Mrs Pearce said, and she started her stopwatch.

I couldn't believe it. No one apart from Sam even remembered that I'd already done the fitness test yesterday. It had to be something to do with Zorelda. It's very important no one at school knows that I'm a witchling or about Coven Road. Zorelda's the only witch I know who is powerful enough to wipe everyone at school's mind clean.

'Okay,' I said, and I ran over to the rope and climbed it right to the top.

As a cat, with my stabilizer whiskers to help me balance, I'd been very good at gym sort of

things yesterday. But Pegatha hadn't had stabilizer whiskers when she was being me and she'd still been good at gym and now I was good at it too.

'Well done, Bella,' Mrs Pearce said, as she ticked the box on my record sheet.

'I knew you could do it,' Sam shouted up to me and he held his thumbs up.

'So did I,' said Angela.

And everyone clapped and cheered as I came back down and did a double cartwheel before running over to jump the vaulting horse and climb the wall bars. Gym was fun!

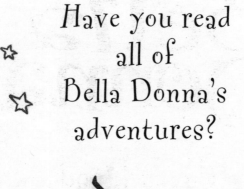

Have you read
all of
Bella Donna's
adventures?

Bella Donna

Coven Road

Most girls dream of being a princess, but
Bella Donna has always longed to be a
witch. The only thing she wants more is
to find a family to take her out of the
children's home where she lives.
But no one seems quite right,
until she meets Lilith.

With Lilith's help, will Bella Donna
be able to make both of her
secret wishes come true?

Bella Donna

Too Many Spells

Bella Donna appears to be a regular girl at a
regular school with her regular friends,
but she has a secret – she is really
a young witch!

She's working hard at learning
her spells, and is desperate to
win the Spell-Casting Contest.
But when strange things start
happening at school, Bella begins
to wonder if she can really
control her magic . . .

Bella Donna

Witchling

Bella Donna is a witchling – a young witch who
must keep her powers a secret, and only
use magic when she's at home in
the enchanted Coven Road.

But it's hard to stick to the rules when magic is
such fun. There are so many things Bella can't
quite resist, like flying on her broomstick and
trying out some very special spells . . .

Bella Donna

Cat Magic

Where is Pegatha?
Bella Donna's favourite cat goes missing and
Bella tries every magic spell she can think of
to find her. All the other witches in Coven
Road get on their broomsticks to join the
search, but with no luck.

There's only one
explanation –
someone must have
put a spell on
Pegatha.
But who,
and why?

Bella Donna

Witch Camp

Bella Donna is off to Witch Camp
for the first time, and there's so much
to look forward to — casting amazing new
spells, sleeping in a treehouse
and toasting marshmallows
over a rainbow fire.
And best of all, Bella's cat
Pegatha will be with her too!
But then things start to go
wrong. Bella realises a spooky
spell has been cast on the fun,
and only she can save the
camp from disaster.

Bella Donna

Join Bella Donna online!

Explore and
download games,
puzzles,
activities,
and much more!

BellaDonnaOnline.co.uk

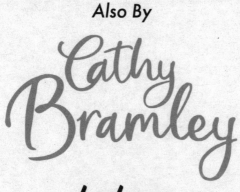

Also By

Cathy Bramley

Ivy Lane

Tilly Parker needs a fresh start, fresh air and a fresh attitude if she is ever to leave the past behind and move on. Seeking out peace and quiet in a new town, will Tilly learn to stop hiding among the sweet peas and let people back into her life – and her heart?

Appleby Farm

Freya Moorcroft is happy with her life, but she still misses the beautiful Appleby Farm of her childhood. Discovering the farm is in serious financial trouble, Freya is determined to turn things around. But will saving Appleby Farm and following her heart come at a price?

Conditional Love

Sophie Stone's life is safe and predictable, just the way she likes it. But then a mysterious benefactor leaves her an inheritance, with one big catch: meet the father she has never seen. Will Sophie be able to build a future on her own terms – and maybe even find love along the way?

Wickham Hall

Holly Swift has landed her dream job: events co-ordinator at Wickham Hall. She gets to organise for a living, and it helps distract from her problems at home. But life isn't quite as easily organised as a Wickham Hall event. Can Holly learn to let go and live in the moment?

The Plumberry School Of Comfort Food

Verity Bloom hasn't been interested in cooking ever since she lost her best friend and baking companion two years ago. But when tragedy strikes at her friend's cookery school, can Verity find the magic ingredient to help, while still writing her own recipe for happiness?

White Lies & Wishes

When unlikely trio Jo, Sarah and Carrie meet by chance, they embark on a mission to make their wishes come true. But with hidden issues, hidden talents and hidden demons, the new friends must admit what they really want if they are ever to get their happy endings . . .

The Lemon Tree Café

Finding herself unexpectedly jobless, Rosie Featherstone begins helping her beloved grandmother at the Lemon Tree Café. But when disaster looms for the café's fortunes, can Rosie find a way to save the Lemon Tree Café and help both herself and Nonna achieve the happy ending they deserve?

Hetty's Farmhouse Bakery

Hetty Greengrass holds her family together, but lately she's full of self-doubt. Taking part in a competition to find the very best produce might be just the thing she needs. But with cracks appearing and shocking secrets coming to light, Hetty must decide where her priorities really lie...

A Match Made In Devon

Nina has always dreamed of being a star, but after a series of very public blunders, she's forced to lay lie in Devon. But soon Nina learns that even more drama can be found in a small village, and when a gorgeous man catches her eye, will Nina still want to return to the bright lights?

A Vintage Summer

Fed up with London, Lottie Allbright takes up the offer of a live-in job managing a local vineyard, Butterworth Wines, where a tragic death has left everyone at a loss. Lottie's determined to save the vineyard, but then she discovers something that will turn her summer – and her world – upside down...